For Christopher Melling

Thanks Dad

HODDER CHILDREN'S BOOKS

First published in Great Britain in 2002 by Hodder and Stoughton
This edition published in 2017

Text and illustrations copyright © David Melling, 2002

The moral rights of the author have been asserted.

A CIP catalogue record for this book
is available from the British Library.

ISBN: 978 1 444 93182 2

10 9 8 7 6 5 4 3 2 1

Printed and bound in China

Hodder Children's Books
An imprint of Hachette Children's Group
Part of Hodder and Stoughton
Carmelite House
50 Victoria Embankment
London EC4Y 0DZ

An Hachette UK Company
www.hachette.co.uk

www.hachettechildrens.co.uk

www.davidmelling.co.uk

JUST LIKE
MY DADDY

DAVID MELLING

Hodder
Children's
Books

This is my daddy.

One day, I'll have sharp teeth...

...just like my daddy.

And spiky hair...

...just like my daddy.

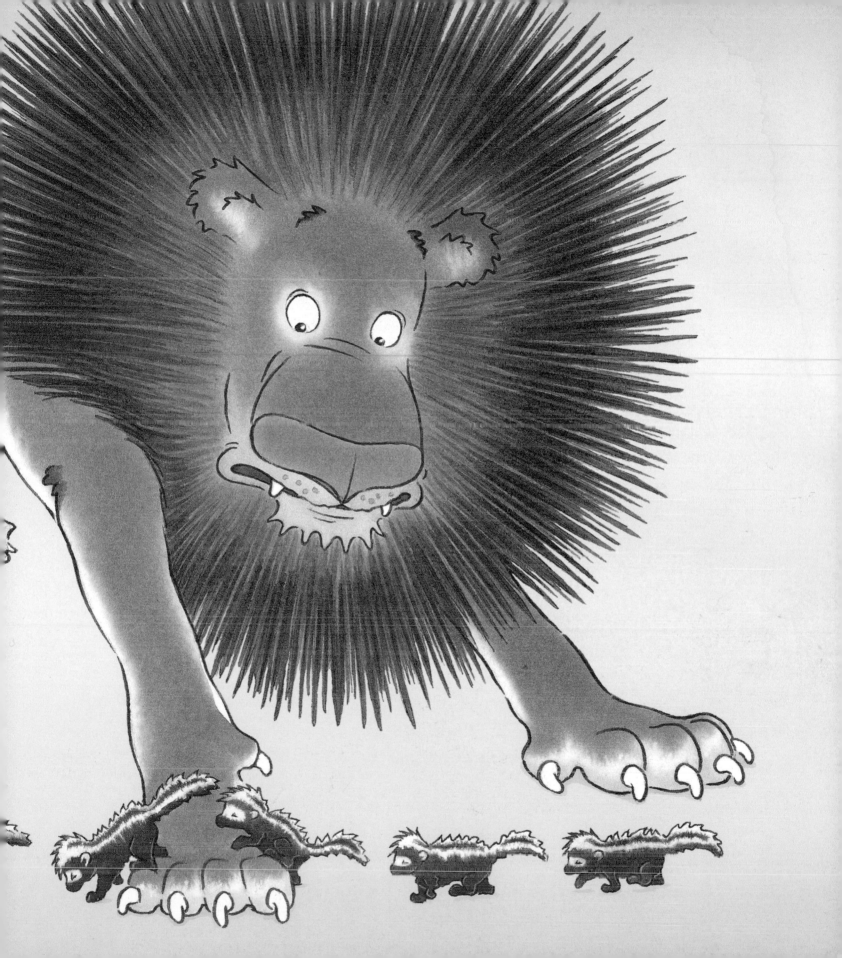

I'll grow long nails
and a swishy tail...

...just like my daddy.

...just like my daddy.

When I eat my tummy talks...

Gurgle
Gurgle

...just like my daddy's.

And when I lie around being

lazy, my mummy says...

My daddy says
I must not be
afraid of
anything...

big. . . .

...or small.

Sometimes my daddy can be a little cross...

...but I try to make him laugh really loud.

When we play
hide-and-seek with my
friends my daddy likes
to go first...

But he's not very good!

Even so, all my friends say
when they grow up they want to be...

...just like my daddy.

LOOK OUT FOR THESE GREAT STORIES STARRING:

HUGLESS DOUGLAS

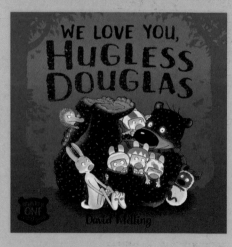

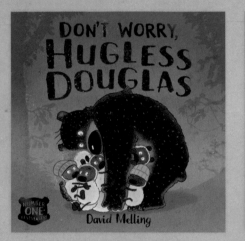

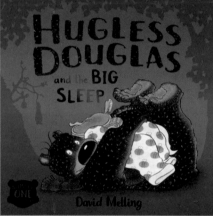

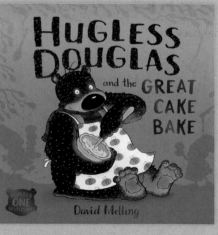

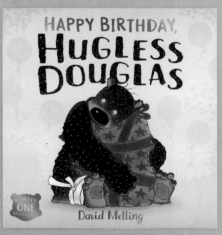

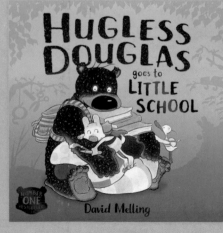